First published 2012 by Macmillan Children's Books
This edition published 2013 by Macmillan Children's Books
a division of Macmillan Publishers Limited
20 New Wharf Road, London N1 9RR
Basingstoke and Oxford. Associated companies throughout the world
www.panmacmillan.com
ISBN: 978-1-4472-1026-9
Text and illustrations copyright © Chloë and Mick Inkpen 2012
Moral rights asserted. All rights reserved.
1 3 5 7 9 8 6 4 2
A CIP catalogue record for this book is available from the British Library.
Printed in China

Hello Oscar!

Zoe and Beans

Chloë & Mick Inkpen

MACMILLAN CHILDREN'S BOOKS

Beans had found something exciting at the bottom of the garden.

It was small and squeaky with tufty hair.

A **guinea pig!**

'Woof!' said Beans.
'Squeak,' said the guinea pig.

And off they went to find a carrot.

When they came back
there was another guinea pig
in the garden!

And a **tortoise!**

Zoe had never seen a real
tortoise before.

'I wonder if it likes carrot too?'
said Zoe.

But Beans had found something
even more interesting . . .

. . . a chameleon!

Wow!

The chameleon began
to change colour!
Its long, thin tongue
poked in and out.
  'Are you hungry?' said Zoe.
'What do chameleons eat?'
she wondered, and she rushed
  inside to Google it.

'Live crickets!'
said Zoe as she came
back outside.
'Where am I
going to find
live...'

. . . There was
a **parrot** in the bush!

'This morning I had
just one pet, and now I've got
   two guinea pigs,
a tortoise,
   a chameleon,
a parrot. . .

   . . .and Beans!'

(But where was Beans?)

'Hello Oscar!' said the parrot.
It was a **talking** parrot!

'My name's Zoe actually,'
said Zoe. 'Can you say, "Hello Zoe."'

'Hello Oscar!'
said the parrot.

It flew further into the garden.

'Hello Zoe,' said Zoe.
'Hello Oscar,' said the parrot.

'Hello Zoe,' said Zoe.
'Hello Oscar,' said the parrot.

'Hello Zoe,' said Zoe.
'Hello Oscar,' said the parrot.

This parrot wasn't as clever
as it looked.

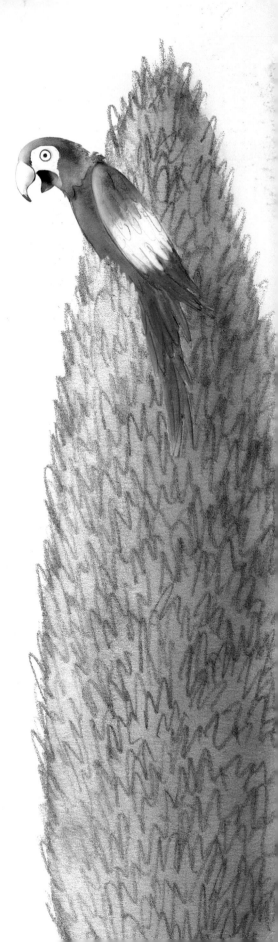

Zoe spelt out the letters.

H e l l o

The parrot looked blank,
then opened its beak and said,

'Hello Oscar'.

Z o e

'My name's not Oscar!

It's Zoe! Zoe! Zoe!'

Woof!
Woof!
Woof!

There was Beans!

And not just Beans.
A rabbit.
A duck.
And a face!
A friendly face.
'Nice dog!'
said the face.

The face disappeared
and a moment later a little
bottom began wiggling
backwards through the hole.
Then a stripey jumper...

. . . and lots and lots of curly hair.

'Hello, I'm Oscar!'

'Hello Oscar!' said Zoe.